This book was given to

..................................................

From

..................................................

On this date

..................................................

*Thank You, Lord, for people who only focus on the wise decisions I make and tell me that's who I truly am. Help me be one of those people to others.*

— J. Rutland

Published in Nashville, Tennessee, by Tommy Nelson. Tommy Nelson is a registered trademark of Thomas Nelson, Inc.

Published in association with the Prospect Agency, Upper Montclair, New Jersey.

Thomas Nelson, Inc., titles may be purchased in bulk for educational, business, fund-raising, or sales promotional use. For information, please e-mail SpecialMarkets@ThomasNelson.com.

**Library of Congress Cataloging-in-Publication Data**

Rutland, Jarrett.
    I love you no matter what : a Prince Chirpio story / by J. Rutland.
        p. cm.
    Summary: In this retelling of the parable of the prodigal son, Prince Chirpio, a young bird, disobeys his father and sets out on an adventure, only to find that leaving home was a very bad decision.
    ISBN 978-1-4003-2195-7 (hardcover)
    [1. Birds—Fiction. 2. Obedience—Fiction. 3. Love—Fiction. 4. Parables.]  I. Title.
    PZ7.R9355Ial 2013
    [E]—dc23

                                        2012029284

*Printed in China*

13 14 15 16 TIMS 6 5 4 3 2 1

# I Love You
# No Matter What

A Prince Chirpio Story

Written and Illustrated
## by J. Rutland

Tommy
NELSON®

A Division of Thomas Nelson Publishers

NASHVILLE   DALLAS   MEXICO CITY   RIO DE JANEIRO

Today had been a bad day. Little Blue had forgotten to clean his nest, he had been mean to his baby sister, and he had spilled his bowl of birdseed. First his father was sad, then he was angry, and finally he just shook his head at his little bluebird.

"Daddy," Little Blue said with a pout, "since you probably don't love me anymore, I'm leaving the big oak tree for good."

"I'm very sorry to hear that," Daddy Blue said patiently. "But before you leave, I'd like to tell you a story of a very special bird much like you. His name was Prince Chirpio."

Far away, in Skinny Tree Kingdom, Prince Chirpio had always liked being royalty. He liked living in the castle and wearing his royal robe. But he didn't like that his father, King Puffbelly, still expected Chirpio to follow certain rules. He was to practice his chirping. He was to save his birdseed pie until after dinner. And he was never to wander beyond the borders of the kingdom.

One night, while Chirpio and his father were pretending to slay dragonflies, Chirpio said, "Father, I'm a brave prince. I should be going on adventures. I should be fighting real dragonflies. I should be rescuing princesses."

"My, my, that's a lot of *shoulds*," replied King Puffbelly. "But I love you too much to let you leave the kingdom just yet, my son. One day you will take your special bag of birdseed I've saved for you, and you'll have an adventure of your own, but for now I'm going to keep your feathers safe here with me."

That night, Chirpio lay in his nest thinking. *I am a brave prince,* he thought. *Finding adventure is much more important than keeping my feathers clean.*

He decided to go ahead and get his bag of birdseed *now* and find a land of excitement where he could make his own rules.

While the rest of the royal family slept, Chirpio tossed the bag of birdseed over his shoulder, tiptoed through the castle gates, and flew off into the darkness.

He flew and he flew.

Then he marched and he marched.

Finally, when his wings and feet were just too tired, he leaned against a rock and fell fast asleep.

Chirpio awoke a few hours later with an empty tummy and worn-out wings. Soon a grasshopper came hopping through the trees.

"I'm Prince Chirpio," the young prince declared. "I need to rest before my big adventure. If I give you some birdseed, will you make a royal nest for me? One fit for a prince?"

"Give me enough seed, and I'll make you a nest fit for a king!" said the grasshopper, and he got to work.

Soon a caterpillar and turtle arrived.

"Could you share some seed with us too?" the turtle asked.

"Well," answered Chirpio, "I'm going on an adventure, and I really need a robe and breakfast. If you will make me a cool royal robe and a giant chocolate birdseed pie, I'll pay you with seed."

So the caterpillar and turtle got to work.

Prince Chirpio soon had a beautiful nest,
a fancy new robe, and a mouth covered in
chocolate birdseed. He and his new friends
spent the next few days lying around,
snacking, and dreaming of adventures.

Meanwhile, back in the Skinny Tree Kingdom, King Puffbelly had realized that Chirpio was gone. He was aflutter with worry over his little prince.

*Chirpio, where are you? Don't you know I miss you?* thought the king. *I'll never stop searching for you, and I'll never stop loving you.*

But Chirpio wasn't thinking about his father. He had been too busy enjoying his giant pie and his fancy robe and nest. His new friends—the grasshopper, the caterpillar, and the turtle—did what he wanted and played with him . . . until one day when Chirpio's bag of birdseed was suddenly empty.

"See ya, Chirpster," said Turtle. "When you have new birdseed, call us. Until then, maybe the pigs in the next pasture will share their food with you." He and his friends laughed to themselves.

Chirpio flew away sadly, feeling lonelier than ever.

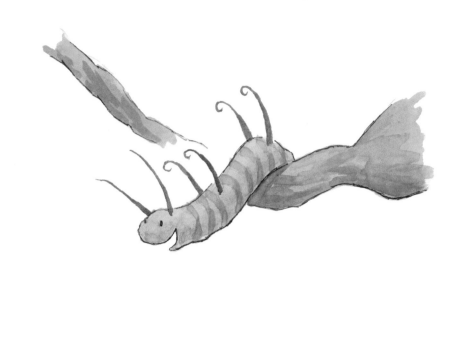

When he flew over the nearby pasture, Chirpio saw the family of pigs having their dinner. He perched on a branch above them to think about what to do next.

*I wonder if the pigs really do have some seed to share,* he thought. He leaned out of the tree to get a better look at the sloppy mess they were eating. *Yuck! But I'm so hungry that I might even be able to eat some of that.*

Even though it looked icky.

And gooey.

And stinky.

And . . .

OOPS! Chirpio lost his balance and fell tail first among the pigs, sending piglets squealing and slop splashing. He sat up in the middle of the muddy, gloopy mess. Stinky slop was running down his head, and Mother Pig was not happy with him.

*That's it*, thought Chirpio. He had wasted his seed. He was hungry. He was lonely. And now he was covered in pig slop. Leaving home had been a very bad decision.

*I don't belong here. I belong in the castle with my father. I'm going home*, he thought. So Chirpio shook off the slop as best as he could and flew off toward Skinny Tree Kingdom. But as he flew, he kept wondering, *I've done such a bad thing. Will my father still love me?*

After hours of flying, Chirpio finally saw his father in the distance. The prince was nervous. What if his father was angry? What if he didn't allow Chirpio back into the kingdom? What if his father didn't love him anymore?

When he landed, the prince bowed his head in front of the king and said, "I'm sorry, Daddy. I understand if you don't want me to come home. Maybe I can just work for you in the castle."

To Chirpio's surprise, King Puffbelly just threw his wings around his son and pulled him into a huge hug.

"Daddy . . . does that mean you still love me? Even though I wasted all the seed you had saved for me? Even though I disobeyed and left the kingdom? Even though I left *you*?"

"I don't like the choices you made," the king answered, "but I'm so happy you came home. Listen carefully, my son. No matter what you do, no matter where you go, I love you no matter what!"

The king had much to celebrate, so the next day he threw a party for the entire kingdom. He even asked the royal chefs to make giant chocolate birdseed pies for everyone, which made Chirpio the happiest bird in the kingdom.

Daddy Blue smiled. "So you see, Little Blue, Prince Chirpio learned that his father would always love him—no matter what he did. Love isn't about actions. Love just is."

Little Blue looked down at his suitcase. "So you still love me—even on days when I forget to do my chores, or I'm not so nice to my sister, or I make a big mess? Even on days when I almost fly away forever?" he asked.

Daddy Blue hugged his little bird. "On fun days and
sad days and happy days and mad days. When you make
mistakes and when you make a mess. I will always love you,
Little Blue . . .

"No matter what."